Yes I Can!

I'm Clover Anne!

written by: Cheryl A. Cunningham, PE & Judith E. Cunningham

illustrated by: Jill M. VanMatre

PCS Engineers Publishing
1924 South Dan Jones Road
Avon, Indiana 46123
317-837-9900

Ordering information:
www.CreateSpace.com/4962789
www.amazon.com

Printed by CreateSpace, An Amazon.com Company

ISBN 978-0-9905344-0-2
Library of Congress Control Number: 2014911794

Book Layout and Design: Erin E. Güt
Fonts: Sassoon Primary, CurlzMT, TamilMN, PWSimpleHandwriting, Noteworthy, Impact

The illustrations in this book were made with watercolor. For page 29, CAD was utilized to create illustrations and graph paper was used for the background.

First Edition, 2014

www.icanbeanengineer.com

This book is dedicated
to our very own
Clover Anne.
We know she can!

Clover Anne looked out her window and watched the rain. She was not happy.

"I want to play on my brand new playground," she said. "It has a slide that goes around and around, 10 bars to climb up and down, swings that go as high as the sky, and a tunnel that is shaped like a dragonfly."

"I know, my dear," said her mother. "But remember what happens to the creek when it rains?"

Clover Anne remembered. That is why she was so glum. Something was wrong with the creek, and something must be done.

Before the playground, the little creek next
to the yard was barely a trickle, even when it rained.

Before the playground, the water flowed
right where it was supposed to go.

But something happened when the workers came to build her playground. The big trucks drove all over the yard and right through the creek! And then, nothing was the same. Nothing.

Now when it rains, the creek floods and the yard becomes a giant lake with a playground right in the middle.

"What good is a playground that has a slide that goes around and around, 10 bars to climb up and down, swings that go as high as the sky, and a tunnel that is shaped like a dragonfly, if it is surrounded by water?" Clover Anne complained. "There must be a way to make the water stay in the creek. Hmmmmmm."

"Mom," moaned Clover Anne. "My playground is great when it's not in a lake, but our creek is a problem, and it needs to be fixed." Mom set her things aside and looked at Clover Anne. "You are clever Clover Anne, I know you can figure out what to do."

So Clover Anne put on her
pink striped raincoat with matching
pink hat and purple boots, and outside she went.
She stood in the rain, stared at the creek,
and thought...

...and thought.
Just when her feet were about to sink into the mud, she suddenly remembered another time she was in the same conundrum.

It was last summer at the beach when Clover Anne and her family built a huge sandcastle. She imagined she was a beautiful Princess and the castle was her grand home. But when the ocean waves crashed onto shore and into her castle, it was nearly flooded!

She desperately needed to save her castle.
She had to keep the water out!
"Hey!" thought Clover Anne excitedly.
"That's what I want to do, keep the water out of the yard."

She saved her castle that day by using lots of sand
to make the wall around the castle higher.

"That was a good idea,"
she remembered. "It was fun. I
made the walls higher, and that made
the water flow where I wanted it to go.
I bet I can do that in my yard!"

Clover Anne ran inside. "Mom, may I borrow some of your paper and a lavender marker, and may I invite five friends over tomorrow?"

"Yes, yes and yes," laughed Mom. "What are you planning?"

"We're going to fix that creek!" exclaimed Clover Anne. "Thanks, Mom!"

The next day Clover Anne's friends came over. "Here's what I think," she explained to them.

"I think the big trucks smashed the side of the
creek. Now the water runs into the yard
and encroaches on the playground."

"Look," she said pointing to her drawing.
"We need to make the sides of the creek higher
just like I did with my sandcastle last summer.
This will make the water flow where we want it to go."

Clover Anne and her friends went outside and hauled and rolled
and pushed and carried rocks and sticks and leaves.
The sides of the creek grew higher and higher.
They even used lots of gooey, sticky mud to
make sure everything stayed in place.
They worked very, very hard,
and when they were
finished, it looked
magnificent!

"Good work, team!"
praised Clover Anne.
"Now all we need is rain!"

Very soon it did rain. Clover Anne
nervously looked out the window and
watched the rain. She watched the creek.
She watched the yard. She watched her
playground with a slide that goes around
and around, 10 bars to climb up and down,
swings that go as high as the sky,
and a tunnel that is shaped like a dragonfly.

Then
something very
magical
happened.

The water stayed in the creek! The creek flowed right where it was supposed to go. The yard did not turn into a lake! The playground was safe!

"Mom!" yelled Clover Anne.
"It worked!"
"Oh my clever Clover Anne,"
Mom said when
she saw what Clover Anne
had accomplished.
"You solved your problem
just like an engineer."

"An engineer?"
asked Clover Anne.
"What is an engineer?"

"Engineers dream, imagine, design, and create,"
explained Mom. "That's what makes their job so great.
They figure out ways to make a creek go straight
so it doesn't turn into a giant lake."

"Whoa, whoa, whoa!..." said Clover Anne,
getting very excited. "It was so much fun!
I can do all those things!
I want to be one!"

Delighted and excited as her
dog with a bow,
she grabbed her boa
and prepared for a show.

I can dream,
imagine,
design, and create...
And I
know how
to do something great!

Oh, I can dream,
imagine,
design and create...
And I
know I
can do something great!

Oh, yes I CAN,
Oh, yes I CAN,
Oh, yes I CAN,
I'm Clover Anne!

Oh, yes I CAN,
Oh, yes I CAN,
Oh, yes I CAN,
I'm Clover Anne!

Then dancing and singing in front
of the mirror she belted out the finale of her premier,
"This announcement is for the whole world to hear!"

I'm
going
to be
an

Engineer!

Our Team

An Engineer,
a Teacher,
and an Artist

Sisters, Cheryl and Judy Cunningham, share a passion for positively influencing children and youth.

As a professional engineer, Cheryl (the engineer) wanted to introduce the fun and excitement of engineering by demonstrating that problem solving in everyday activities is what engineers do!

As an educator, literacy advocate, and writer Judy (the teacher) joined the team to create stories about engineering for young children.

Judy's daughter, Jill VanMatre (the artist), captured the essence of the stories with sketch, watercolor, and technology. Jill's daughter, the real-life, Clover Anne, completed the team by inspiring everyone to believe that "Yes, I Can!"

Yes I Can, I'm Clover Anne is the first book in a collection of stories, *I Can Be An Engineer*, written for young children.

xoxo, Lola

You can

Ride your , walk your , watch ,

your mom, play video games, to visit

grandma, take a to school, drink clean

water, take a , flush the , have clean

, play on the , go to the ,

listen to , turn on a , eat an , work on

your computer, with your friends,

have lights in your shoes, play at night,

and read this book...

.... thanks to an Engineer!

Engineers dream, imagine, design and create.
That's what makes their job so great.
Finding solutions is what they do
To make the world better for me and for you.

Made in the USA
Middletown, DE
28 January 2016